· The ·
ORCHARD
· Book of ·
MAGICAL
TALES

· ALSO · IN · THIS · SERIES ·

The Orchard Book of Nursery Rhymes
Faith Jaques

•

The Orchard Book of Nursery Stories
Sophie Windham

•

The Orchard Book of Fairy Tales
Retold by *Rose Impey*
Illustrated by *Ian Beck*

•

The Orchard Books of Greek Myths
Retold by *Geraldine McCaughrean*
Illustrated by *Emma Chichester Clark*

•

The Orchard Book of Funny Poems
Compiled by *Wendy Cope*
Illustrated by *Amanda Vesey*

•

The Orchard Books of Poems for Children
Compiled by *Adrian Mitchell*

· The ·
ORCHARD
· Book of ·
MAGICAL
T A L E S

· Retold by ·
MARGARET MAYO

· Illustrated by ·
JANE RAY

ORCHARD BOOKS

To Peter
M.M.

To Ben Horsburgh
J.R.

ORCHARD BOOKS
96 Leonard Street
London EC2A 4RH
Orchard Books Australia
14 Mars Road, Lane Cove, NSW 2066
1 85213 383 X
First published in Great Britain in 1993
Text © Margaret Mayo 1993
Illustrations © Jane Ray 1993
The right of Margaret Mayo to be identified as author and of Jane Ray
as illustrator of this work has been asserted by them in accordance
with the Copyright, Designs and Patents Act, 1988.
A CIP catalogue record for this book is available
from the British Library.
Printed in Malaysia by Times Offset (M)

Contents

· THE · LEMON · PRINCESS ·

Once, in the faraway times when toads had wings and camels could fly, there lived a king and queen who had an only son called Prince Omar; and a time came when they decided that he must do what every other prince did. He must find a beautiful girl and marry her. So Prince Omar looked for a beautiful wife, but—and it was a big but—he could not find a girl who was beautiful enough.

Then, one day, an old woman came to him and said, "My lord prince, let me tell you about a princess—an exceedingly beautiful princess—whose face has not yet been seen by the sun. She is the one you seek. She is your fate."

"How can I find her?" he asked.

"You must ride eastwards for three days and three nights," said the old woman, "and then you will come to a garden hedged around with roses, where there grows a lemon tree that bears three ripe lemons. Pick the lemons, but then be careful and do not cut them open until you come to a place where there is plenty of water.''

So the next morning Prince Omar mounted his horse and set off. He rode eastwards for three days and three nights, until he came to a garden hedged around with roses. He opened the gate and walked in. He looked all around and he found the lemon tree that had three ripe lemons. So he picked them and rode off, back the way he had come.

Now he had not gone far when he began to wonder what was inside those lemons, so he chose one, took a knife and cut it open. And there rose up from the lemon an exceedingly beautiful girl. "Water!" she called out. "Please give me water!"

But there was no water anywhere; and the next moment the girl faded away, and she was gone.

Prince Omar was sad. But the thing was done, and there was no going back. So on he rode.

It was not long, however, before he began to wonder about the other two lemons and whether there were girls in them also. So he chose another one, took his knife and cut it open. And there rose up from the lemon a girl who was even more beautiful than the first, and she called out, "Water! Please give me water!"

But again there was no water anywhere; and the girl faded away, and she was gone.

"I see now that I must take great care of my third lemon," said the prince. And on he rode.

After a while he came to a river, and, remembering the old woman's advice, he took the third lemon and cut it open. And there rose up a girl who was even more beautiful than the two who had come before—eyes gentle as the moon, skin pale as ivory, and hair long, shiny black and soft as silk. And she too called out, "Water! Please give me water!"

Well, Prince Omar was so anxious not to lose this beautiful girl that he took hold of her and dropped her straight into the river. Just like that. And she drank the clear, fresh water until she was satisfied, and then she climbed out, all naked as she was.

The prince took off his cloak and wrapped it round her. "My beautiful Lemon Princess, you, and you alone, shall be my bride," he said. "But, before I take you to the palace, I must go and fetch some fine clothes for you to wear and a horse for you to ride."

"Then I shall hide in this tall poplar tree, until you return," said the Lemon Princess. And with that she called out, "Bend down, tall tree! Bend down!"

Immediately the tree bent down and she seated herself on the topmost branch, and the tree stood tall again. And then Prince Omar rode off.

Time comes, time goes, and the Lemon Princess sat high in the tree and waited. After a while, a servant girl—an ugly girl, with mean eyes, tangled hair and rough skin—came to fill her water jar at the river. As she bent down, she saw the face of the beautiful Lemon Princess reflected in the clear water.

"There—see how beautiful I am!" she cried. "I always knew I was far too beautiful to be a servant!"

Then she heard someone laugh and a voice call out, "Look up, not down!"

So the servant girl looked up, and when she saw the Lemon Princess sitting at the very top of the poplar tree, she said, "What are you doing up there in that tall tree?"

The Lemon Princess answered, "I am waiting for my bridegroom, the royal prince, to return with fine clothes for me to wear and a horse for me to ride."

Then the servant girl thought some wicked thoughts and she said, "O lady, lovely lady, let me come up and talk to you and help pass the weary hours while you wait."

The Lemon Princess was lonely, so she said, "Bend down, tall tree! Bend down!" And the tree bent down, and the servant girl was soon up amongst the topmost branches.

"O lady, lovely lady," said the servant girl, "who are you with your magic powers? Are you human? Or are you a peri maiden from the land of enchantment?"

The Lemon Princess answered, "I was once a peri maiden, but now I have chosen to enter the world of humans and to become the Lemon Princess."

"O lady, lovely lady, let me comb your long black hair." And the servant girl began to comb the Lemon Princess's hair and then—and then she found a hairpin stuck deep in her long black hair.

"O lady, lovely lady, what is this?" she asked.

"It is my talisman," said the Lemon Princess. "Do not touch it."

Immediately the servant girl pulled out the hairpin, and *whir-r-r-r!* the Lemon Princess changed into a white dove, fluttered her wings and flew up and away.

Then the servant girl took off her own clothes, threw them into the river below and they floated away. Then she wrapped the prince's cloak around her and waited.

Now when Prince Omar returned and saw the ugly servant girl in the poplar tree, he was amazed.

"What has happened?" he cried. "You have changed. Your skin is rough and dry."

"It was the sun, my lord," she said. "The scorching sun burnt it."

"But your lips? Your lips that were soft as rosebuds. What about them?"

"It was the wind, my lord," she said. "The hot dry wind cracked them."

"But your eyes that were so large and gentle?"

"It was the tears, my lord," she said. "The tears I wept because I thought you would never return have made them red and swollen."

"But your hair that was soft as silk?"

"It was the black crow, my lord," she said. "The black crow tried to build a nest in my hair and tangled it and made it rough."

Then the ugly servant girl climbed down from the tree and said, "Time is a great healer, my lord. Soon I shall be as I was before."

And Prince Omar believed her. He gave her beautiful clothes to wear—bag trousers, blue as the summer sky, a white silk blouse embroidered with pearls, a jacket of gold thread, gold slippers, a gold head-dress and gold bangles. And then, together, they rode off to the palace.

Well, when Prince Omar took the servant girl to meet the king and queen, they saw at once how ugly she was and they said, "*This* is your chosen bride! Surely not!"

"I have given her my word," said the prince. "And in forty days our marriage will be celebrated."

Now there was a garden around the king's palace, and every morning a white dove came and sat upon a sandalwood tree and sang. Every day Prince Omar came and stood beneath the tree and listened, and every day he said, "How sad is the song that the white dove sings!"

As soon as the servant girl noticed this, she went to the gardener and said, "The prince commands you to catch the white dove that sings the sad song in the sandalwood tree and kill it and bury it deep in the ground."

And the gardener killed the bird and buried it.

But the next day, at the very place where the dove was buried, there sprang up a great cypress tree, and the wind came and sighed in its branches.

When Prince Omar saw the tree he was astonished. "What wonder is this!" he said. "A cypress where no tree stood before." And when he heard the wind sighing, he said, "How sad is the sound of the wind in its branches!"

Then the servant girl went to the gardener and said, "The prince commands you to cut down the cypress tree and make from its wood a cradle for the son which one day I shall give him. Take any wood that remains and burn it."

And the gardener cut down the tree, and the palace carpenters cut the wood into planks and made a cradle. Then the gardener gathered all the wood that remained and built a fire. He was just going to throw the last small branch on to the flames, when the prince's old nurse went by and asked him for some firewood, so he gave her the small branch from the cypress tree.

Now the old nurse put the branch down beside the fireplace in her house, while she went off to market. The moment she shut the door, the branch shivered all over and—well! it changed into a girl. An exceedingly beautiful girl. The Lemon Princess herself.

At once she set to work. She swept the floor. She washed the dishes. She peeled vegetables and cooked a meal. And then she hid behind a door.

When the old nurse returned, she *was* surprised. "Who has done all this?" she said. "A human or one of the peri kind?"

Then the Lemon Princess came out from her hiding place and she said, "I cleaned and I cooked for you, and now, I ask you, will you do something for me? Go to Prince Omar and tell him that there lives in your house a girl who can make fine carpets, and if he will give you silk threads, she will make for him the finest carpet ever seen."

The old nurse went and spoke to the prince, and he ordered that she should be given silk threads and anything else that was needed. So then the Lemon Princess set to work on her carpet.

Time comes, time goes. The day came when Prince Omar was to marry the wicked servant girl. She had not changed: she was as ugly as ever. But the prince said to himself, "Surely she *is* the Lemon Princess—the one who is my fate. Besides, I have given my word, and so I must marry her."

But early in the morning of that very day, the old nurse brought the finished carpet to the prince and said, "My lord prince, here is a wedding gift!"

Prince Omar unrolled the carpet and he looked; and there was a picture of a garden hedged all around with roses, and in the centre of the garden was a portrait of the Lemon Princess.

"Who made this carpet?" asked the prince.

"A girl who lives with me," she answered.

"Bring her to me," he said.

So the Lemon Princess came to the palace; and the moment Prince Omar saw her, he knew her.

"Truly," he said, "you alone are my beautiful Lemon Princess— my fate—the one who must be my bride. But, tell me, where have you been? What happened to you these long and weary days?"

Then the Lemon Princess told him about the wicked servant girl and all her evil deeds. And the prince was angry and sent his guards to find the servant girl. But as soon as she heard that she had been discovered, she was up and off, with the guards at her heels. And she kept running until she was over the border and into the next kingdom. Some say she's running still!

But then, at last, there was a wedding, and Prince Omar married the beautiful Lemon Princess. And for seven days and seven nights the pipes were played, the drums rolled and there was feasting, dancing and great merriment.

Persian

· FEATHER · WOMAN · AND · THE · ·MORNING·STAR·

One night in the moon of flowers, the time when the wild rose blooms and the grass is long upon the prairie, a girl called Feather Woman and her young sister took their blankets and slept outside their lodge. Just before dawn Feather Woman woke and saw the morning star rising in the east; and it was so beautiful that she could not take her eyes off it.

"Wake up! And look over there at the morning star!" she called to her sister. "How I do love that star. It is the brightest and best of them all!"

Her sister laughed and teasing her said, "So—you would like to marry a star!"

"It is true," Feather Woman answered quietly. "I would marry the morning star."

A few days later Feather Woman was on her way to the river to fetch some water, when she met a stranger on the trail. He was tall and straight and more handsome than any man she had ever seen. He wore clothes of soft tanned skin that smelt of pine and sweet grass. There was a yellow plume in his hair, and he was holding a branch of juniper that had a spider's web hanging from it.

"I am Morning Star," he said. "One night I saw you lying in the long grass and heard your words of love. Now I ask you to leave your camp and come to the Above World and live there together with me."

Feather Woman trembled as she heard these words. She said, "First let me go to my mother and father and say goodbye. And then I will come with you."

But he answered, "You must come now or not at all."

And he took the yellow plume and fastened it in her hair. Then he offered her the branch of juniper and said, "Take this and close your eyes. The spider ladder will carry you to my home."

So Feather Woman took the juniper and closed her eyes; and when she opened them again she was in the sky, standing before a great lodge.

"Welcome to my home," said Morning Star. "This is the lodge of my father, the Sun, and my mother, the Moon."

Now at that time the Sun was away on his travels, but the kindly Moon was there. And she welcomed her son's new bride. She offered her food and drink, and then gave her a soft tanned buckskin dress, a bracelet of elk teeth and an elk-skin robe, decorated with secret paintings.

The days passed by, and Feather Woman was happy in the Above World. The Moon showed her the abundance of flowers and vegetables and berries that grew there, and taught her about herbs and secret medicines. She also gave her a digging stick made of wood hardened in fire and showed her how to use the stick to dig up the many wild roots that could be eaten.

But the Moon warned Feather Woman that there was one plant she must never dig up. It was the Giant Turnip that grew near the lodge of the Spider Man, who wove the ladders by which the star people travelled between earth and sky. The Moon told Feather Woman many times, "The Giant Turnip is sacred. If you touch it, you will bring unhappiness to us all."

Time passed, and Morning Star and Feather Woman had a baby son, and they called him Star Boy; and it seemed then that their happiness was complete.

But one day when Feather Woman was out with her digging stick, collecting wild vegetables, she happened to pass the Giant Turnip.

And she said to herself, "I wonder what lies beneath the Giant Turnip."

She walked around it. Then she bent down and examined it closely. And then she laid the baby on the ground and began to dig under the turnip. She dug and she dug, but the turnip would not move. She dug some more, and the digging stick stuck fast underneath. Then she looked up and saw two cranes flying overhead.

She called to them, "Come, mighty cranes! Come and help me move the Giant Turnip!"

They circled above her three times and then they landed. They took hold of the turnip with their long, sharp beaks and rocked it to and fro. They sang a magic song and rocked it again until *prrr . . . mm!* it rolled out of the ground, leaving a hole where it had been growing.

Feather Woman knelt down and looked through the hole, and she saw the camp of the Blackfeet Indians where once she had lived. Smoke was rising from the lodges. Children were laughing. Young men were playing games. And the women were working—tanning hides and building lodges, gathering berries on the hills and fetching water from the river.

Then Feather Woman longed to be back again upon the green prairie with her own people. Slowly she got to her feet. She shook her head and she sighed, and when she turned to go home, there were tears in her eyes.

As soon as Morning Star saw her, he knew what she had done. He said, "You have dug up the Giant Turnip!" And that was all he said. Nothing more.

When the Moon heard what had happened, she was sad. But when the Sun heard, he was angry.

He said, "Feather Woman has disobeyed my command, and now she must return to earth. She has looked again upon her own people, and she can no longer be happy here with us."

So Morning Star took his wife and his baby son to the lodge of the Spider Man, and he asked the Spider Man to weave a ladder that would take them down to earth. Then Morning Star placed a digging stick in Feather Woman's hands and wrapped her and Star Boy in an elk-skin robe.

"Close your eyes," he said. "And now, farewell."

It was one evening, in the time when the berries are ripe, that Feather Woman and Star Boy came to earth. People on the prairie looked up and saw a bright falling star. They ran to the place where it landed and found a strange bundle. When they opened the bundle, they saw a girl and a baby. And they knew at once that she was the girl who, many moons before, had gone to fetch water, and had not returned.

From that time on Feather Woman and Star Boy lived in her parents' lodge. And she shared with the Blackfeet Indians all the knowledge she had brought from the Above World. She taught them the secrets of the medicine plants. She showed them how to make a digging stick and how to recognise the wild turnip, the wild onion and other plants that were good to eat.

But Feather Woman never forgot the Above World. And often on clear days, when the sun shone, she would climb to the top of a high ridge and look up into the sky and think of her husband, the great and glorious Morning Star.

North American Indian

· THE · KINGDOM · UNDER · THE · SEA ·

One summer evening, long ago, a lad called Urashima Taro was walking across the beach after a day's fishing when he saw a turtle lying helpless on its back, slowly waving its flippers. So he bent down and picked it up.

"You poor creature," he said, "I wonder who turned you upside down and left you here to die in the sun? Some thoughtless young children who knew no better, I suppose."

He carried the turtle over the sands and waded out into the sea, as deep as he could, before lowering it into the water. And as he let it go, he called out, "Off you go, venerable turtle—and may you live for a thousand years!"

The next morning Urashima rowed out in his boat, as usual, throwing his fishing line as he went. When he had passed the other boats, and was a long way out at sea and all alone, he took a rest

and let the boat drift on the waves.

It was then that he heard someone softly calling: "Urashima! Urashima Taro!"

He looked round, but there was not another boat in sight. Then he heard again: "Urashima! Urashima Taro!" It seemed to come from close by. So he looked again, and then he saw a turtle, swimming beside the boat.

"Turtle," he said, "was it you who called my name just now?"

"Yes, honourable fisherman, I was the one who spoke," answered the turtle. "Yesterday you saved my life, and today I have come to thank you and offer to take you to Ryn Jin, the palace of the Dragon King under the Sea, who is my father."

Urashima was astonished. "The Dragon King under the Sea is your father!" he said. "Surely not!"

"It is true. I am his daughter," she answered. "And if you climb on my back, I will take you to him."

Urashima thought that it would be a fine thing to see the kingdom under the sea, so he climbed out of the boat and sat himself down on the turtle's back.

Immediately they were off, skimming across the waves. And when it seemed they could go no faster, the turtle dived down into the depths of the sea. For a long time they sped through the water, passing whales and sharks, playful dolphins and shoals of silvery fish. At last Urashima saw in the distance a magnificent coral gate decorated with pearls and glittering gems, and beyond it the long sloping roofs and gables of a coral palace.

"We are approaching the gateway of my father's palace," said the turtle, and even as she spoke they reached it. "Now, from here, please, you must walk."

She turned to a swordfish who was the keeper of the gate and said, "This is an honoured guest from the land of Japan. Please show him the way to go." And with that she swam off.

And the swordfish led Urashima into an outer courtyard where a great company of fish, row upon row of octopus and cuttlefish, bonito and plaice, bowed graciously towards him.

"Welcome to Ryn Jin, the palace of the Dragon King under the Sea!" they chorused. "Welcome and thrice welcome!"

Then the great company of fish escorted Urashima through to an inner courtyard that led to the great door of the coral palace. The door opened and there stood a radiantly beautiful princess. She wore flowing garments of red and green, shot through with all the colours of a wave with sunlight on it, and her long black hair streamed over her shoulders in the style of long ago.

"I welcome you to my father's kingdom," she said, "and ask you to stay here for a while in the land of everlasting youth, where summer never dies and sorrow never comes."

As Urashima listened to her words and gazed at her beautiful face, a feeling of contentment flooded over him. "My only wish is that I might stay here with you in this land for ever," he said.

"Then I shall be your bride and we shall live together always," said the princess. "But first we must ask my father for his permission."

And the princess took him by the hand and led him through long corridors to her father's great hall. There they knelt before the mighty lord, the Dragon King under the Sea, and bowed so low that their foreheads touched the floor.

"Honourable father," said the princess, "this is the youth who saved my life in the land of men, and, if it pleases you, he is the one whom I have chosen to be my husband."

"It pleases me," the Dragon King answered, "but what does the fisher-lad say? Does he accept?"

"Oh . . . I gladly accept," said Urashima.

So then there was a wedding feast. And when the princess and Urashima had pledged their love, three times three, with a wedding cup of saké wine, the entertainments began. Soft music was played, and strange and wonderful rainbow-coloured fish danced and sang.

The next day, when the celebrations were over, the princess showed Urashima some of the marvels of her father's coral palace and his kingdom, and the greatest of these was the garden of the four seasons.

To the east lay the garden of spring, where the plum and cherry were in full blossom and birds of all kinds sang sweetly. To the south the trees were clothed in the green of summer and the crickets chirruped lazily. In the west the autumn maples were ablaze with flame-coloured leaves and the chrysanthemums bloomed. While in the north stood the winter garden where the bamboos and the earth were covered in snow, and the ponds were thick with ice.

Now there were so many things to see and wonder at in the kingdom under the sea that Urashima forgot about his own home and his old life. But after a few days, he remembered his parents.

He said to the princess, "By now my mother and father must think that I have been drowned at sea. It must be three days or more since I left them. I must go, immediately, and tell them what has happened."

"Wait," she said. "Wait a little longer. Stay at least one more day, here with me."

"It is my duty to go and see my parents," he answered. "But I will return to you."

"Then I must become a turtle again and carry you to the land above the waves," she said. "But, before you leave, accept this gift from me." And the princess gave him a beautiful, three-tiered lacquer box, tied round with a red silk cord.

"Keep this box with you always, but do not open it, whatever happens."

And Urashima promised that he would not open the box.

Once again the princess became a turtle, Urashima sat astride her back, and they were off. For a long time they rode through the sea, and then, at last, they soared upwards and reached the waves. Urashima turned his face towards the land and saw again the mountains and the bay he knew so well. They came to the beach, and he stepped ashore.

"Remember," said the turtle. "Do not open the box."

"I will remember," he said.

He walked across the sands and took the path that led to his home. But as he looked around, a strange fear came over him. The trees somehow looked different. So did the houses. And he didn't recognise anyone he saw. When he reached his own house, it too looked different. Only the little stream in the garden and a few stepping stones were the same.

He called: "Mother! Father!" And an old man whom he had never seen before opened the door.

"Who are you?" asked Urashima. "And where are my mother and father? And what has happened to our house? Everything has changed. And yet it is only three days, since I, Urashima Taro, lived here."

"This is my house," said the old man, "and it was my father's and my father's father's before him. But I have heard that a man called Urashima Taro once lived here. The story goes that one day he went fishing and didn't come back, and then, not long after, his old parents died of sorrow. But that was about three hundred years ago."

Urashima shook his head. It was hard to believe that his mother and father, and all his friends too, had died long, long ago. He thanked the old man and walked slowly back to the shore and sat down on the sands.

He felt sad. "Three hundred years," he thought. "Three hundred years must be only three days in the kingdom under the sea."

Now as he sat there, he held the lacquer box the princess had given him in his hands, and his fingers idly played with the red silk cord. And the cord came undone. Without thinking what he was doing, he opened the first box. Three soft wisps of smoke came swirling out and curled around him; and the handsome youth became an old, old man. He opened the second box. There was a

mirror inside it; and he looked and he saw that his hair was grey and his face was old and wrinkled. He opened the third box. A crane's feather drifted out, brushed across his face and settled on his head; and the old man changed into a bird—a beautiful and elegant crane.

The crane flew up and looked out over the sea, and he saw a turtle, floating on the waves, close to the shore. The turtle looked up, and she saw the crane. And then she knew that her husband, Urashima Taro, would never ever return to her father's kingdom under the sea.

Japanese

·Unanana · And · The · Enormous ·
·One-Tusked · Elephant ·

Here is a story—a story about Unanana who one day decided to build a house for herself and her two children, a little boy and a little girl. And she built her house, and she built it well. *But* she built the house in the middle of a wide road, and that road was the animals' road through the bush.

Everyone said, "You can't live there. That is the elephants' road . . . the leopards' road . . . the antelopes' road. All the animals use that road. It is a dangerous place."

But Unanana said, "This is a good place to live. I am Unanana and I am not afraid."

Now Unanana's children were beautiful. *Everyone* who saw them said, "Unanana, you have remarkably beautiful children."

And she always answered, "That is true. They are beautiful, and I love them better than anything in the world."

One morning Unanana had to go into the bush to collect fire-wood, so she asked the children's big cousin, who was staying with them for a few days, to look after the little boy and the little girl. And all three went out and played together on the road while Unanana went off into the bush.

Not long after, a shy, gentle-eyed antelope came leaping along the road, and when she saw the children, she asked, "Whose children are those?"

And Big Cousin answered, "They are Unanana's children."

"Oh!" said the antelope. "They are beautiful, beautiful children!" And she went on her way.

A little while later a bold, yellow-eyed leopard came prowling along the road, and when she saw the children, she asked, "Whose children are those?"

And Big Cousin answered, "They are Unanana's children."

"Oh!" said the leopard. "They are beautiful, beautiful children!" And she too went on her way.

Then, a little while later, an enormous, one-tusked elephant came trampling along the road, and when he saw the children, he asked, "Whose children are those?"

And Big Cousin answered, "They are Unanana's children."

"Au! Au!" trumpeted the elephant. "They are beautiful, beautiful children! But they are playing in the middle of MY road!"

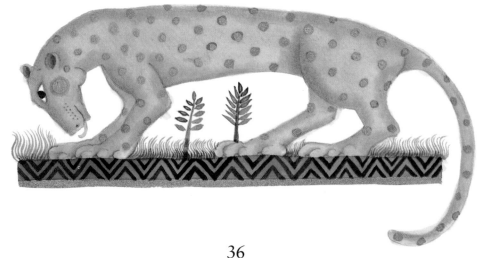

And—next thing—he stretched out his long trunk and picked up the little boy and swooshed him right into his mouth. *Gulp! gulp!* he swallowed him whole. Then he stretched out that long trunk again and picked up the little girl and swooshed her right into his mouth. *Gulp! gulp!* he swallowed her whole. And, yet again, he stretched out that long trunk. But Big Cousin wasn't there. Fast, fast, *very fast* she had run into the house and closed the door behind her.

Then, swinging his long, stretchy trunk from side to side, the enormous, one-tusked elephant went on his way.

When Unanana came home with the firewood, the first thing she noticed was that her children were not playing outside. She went into the house, and there was Big Cousin hunched up in a corner, crying.

"Where are my beautiful children?" asked Unanana.

"They have been taken by an enormous, one-tusked elephant," said Big Cousin.

"What did he do with them?" asked Unanana.

"He ate them," said Big Cousin.

"Did he swallow them whole?" asked Unanana.

"I don't know," said Big Cousin.

Then Unanana ground some maize and mixed it with some milk and cooked a delicious creamy porridge in a large pot. And when the porridge had cooled, she put the pot full of porridge on her head, picked up a big, sharp knife and off she went.

She marched along the animals' road, and she marched and she marched, until she met a shy, gentle-eyed antelope.

"Good mother antelope," said Unanana, "where can I find the enormous, one-tusked elephant that has eaten my beautiful children?"

And the antelope said, "You must go and go and keep going until you come to the place of tall trees and white stones."

So Unanana marched along the animals' road, and she marched and she marched, until she met a bold, yellow-eyed leopard.

"Good mother leopard," she said, "where can I find the enormous, one-tusked elephant that has eaten my beautiful children?"

And the leopard said, "You must go and go and keep going until you come to the place of tall trees and white stones."

So Unanana marched along the animals' road, and she marched and she marched, until she saw an enormous, one-tusked elephant lying down under some tall trees, and all around him were piles of white stones.

Unanana marched up to the elephant and she said, "Are you the elephant that ate my beautiful children?"

The elephant said, "No, I am not the one! Go and go and keep going, and you will find the elephant."

Unanana shouted, "*Are you the elephant that ate my beautiful children?*"

The elephant said, "No, of course I am not the one! Go and go and keep going, and you will find the elephant."

Then Unanana bellowed, "ARE YOU THE ELEPHANT THAT ATE MY BEAUTIFUL CHILDREN?"

And the elephant, still lying on the ground, stretched out his long trunk and picked up Unanana and swooshed her right into his mouth. *Gulp! gulp!* he swallowed her whole, together with the pot full of delicious creamy porridge and the big, sharp knife.

When Unanana got inside the elephant, she *was* surprised. The place was full of dogs, goats, cattle and a whole lot of people—just sitting there, all slumpish and sorry for themselves.

But Unanana didn't sit down. She marched up and down, round and round, inside the elephant, until—*such great happiness!*—she found her two beautiful children sitting next to each other, holding hands.

"Have you had anything to eat?" she asked.

"No," they said, both together. "And we are so hungry."

"Well," said Unanana, "I have brought you some delicious creamy porridge."

By the time the children had eaten as much porridge as they wanted, every single person and every single animal inside the elephant had jumped up and gathered round. They were very hungry. So Unanana shared out the rest of the food; and there was some for everyone.

Now, what with Unanana marching up and down and all the people and animals jumping up and gathering round her, the enormous, one-tusked elephant began to feel uncomfortable.

"Stop moving around down there!" he shouted. "You're giving me a pain in the stomach!"

Unanana said, "Stop moving, indeed! Come on, everybody, let's dance!"

So then the dogs, the goats, the cattle and all the people began to dance.

"Au! Au!" trumpeted the elephant. He had such a big pain in his stomach. "Au! Au! Au! Stop dancing down there!"

But they danced and danced.

The elephant thought to himself, "Since the moment I swallowed that woman, I haven't had any peace! This is too much!" And he shouted, "Get out, all of you! Get out!"

"And how can we get out?" Unanana called back.

"Any way you like!" shouted the elephant. "That's how!"

Then Unanana said, "There is only one way." And she took her big, sharp knife and cut a doorway in the side of the elephant.

And out skipped the dogs and the goats and the cattle, barking and bleating and mooing; and out skipped all the people, laughing. They were so glad to see the grass and the trees and the sky again.

The animals all thanked Unanana for saving them, and hurried off home. And then the people thanked her. But, before hurrying home, they all promised to come and visit her one day at her house in the middle of the animals' road.

Meanwhile, the enormous, one-tusked elephant just lay there, and even though he had a wound in his side he was glad to see those animals and people—most especially Unanana!—hurrying away. He didn't want to see them ever again. They had given him such a big pain in his stomach.

When Unanana and her two children came home and saw Big Cousin there was *such great happiness*! Then Unanana ground some maize and mixed it with some milk and cooked another pot of delicious creamy porridge, and they sat down together and ate it. And it did taste good.

From then on, it was never quiet at Unanana's house, because the people she had met inside the elephant, and the parents of the children who had been there, all came to visit her. And every time they came, they brought presents—a cow or a goat—something like that. And so Unanana and her beautiful children became rich.

But they still lived in their house in the middle of the animals' road. Unanana liked it there. And the enormous one-tusked elephant? He never ever came back.

African (Zulu)

· KATE · CRACKERNUTS ·

Long, long ago, there lived a bonnie princess and her name was Kate. Now it happened that her mother died, and when her father married again, the new queen already had a daughter of her own, and her name also was Kate. So there they were—two Kates in the same family. And it would have been confusing, if it wasn't that the king's Kate was by far the bonnier of the two. So nearly everyone called her Bonnie Kate, while the queen's daughter they called Kate. Just Kate.

Right from the start, the two Kates were friends and loved one another like true sisters. But the queen was bitterly jealous of Bonnie Kate's handsome looks and full of anger that the king's daughter was bonnier than her own. One day she could bear it no longer and went to see the hen-wife, an old witch who kept a flock of hens not far from the castle gates. And the queen asked her to cast a spell on the king's daughter that would spoil her beauty.

"Send the lassie to me," said the hen-wife, "without a bite to eat or a drop to drink, and I'll soon hash up her bonnie face."

So, early next morning, the queen sent the king's daughter to the hen-wife to fetch a basket of eggs for breakfast. But on her way through the kitchen, Bonnie Kate saw some oatcakes on the table, and she picked one up and off she went munching it.

When she came to the hen-wife's house and asked for the eggs, the hen-wife said, "Now lift the lid off that pot there and see what you can see."

Bonnie Kate lifted the lid off the black pot that hung over the fire, and a cloud of steam rose up. A cloud of steam and nothing more.

And the hen-wife said, "Go home to the queen and tell her to keep her larder door better locked!"

Well, next morning the queen once again sent Bonnie Kate to fetch a basket of eggs. She went through the kitchen, and the table was bare. She tried the larder, and the door was locked. But as she walked along the road, she saw an old man picking peas, and being a friendly lass she stopped for a chat. Then the old man gave her a handful of pods, and off she went munching peas.

When Bonnie Kate came to the hen-wife's house and asked for the eggs, the hen-wife said, "Lift the lid off that pot there and see what you can see."

So Bonnie Kate lifted the lid off the black pot, and a cloud of steam rose up. A cloud of steam and nothing more.

And the hen-wife said, "Go home to the queen and tell her that if she wants something done, she must come herself!"

Well, next morning the queen herself woke Bonnie Kate and didn't let her out of sight; and she kept beside her every step of the way to the hen-wife's house.

When they got there, once again the hen-wife said, "Now lift the lid off that pot there and see what you can see."

Bonnie Kate lifted the lid, and then . . . a sheep's head rose up out of the pot and jumped on to her shoulders and covered her own bonnie head entirely. So there she was with a sheep's head instead of her own.

Then the queen was satisfied.

But the other Kate, the queen's own daughter, was angry—very angry—when she saw what had happened to her sister, and said to her, "We can no longer stay here! Who knows what may happen to you next!" And she picked up a fine linen cloth, wrapped it round her sister's head, and took her by the hand. Then together they set out to seek their fortune.

They walked far, they walked further than far, until they came at last to another kingdom. Then Kate went boldly to the king's castle and found work as a kitchen maid; and, in return, she and her sick sister were given food and allowed to sleep in a small room in the attic.

Now the king had two sons, and the elder of the two was ill and no one knew what ailed him. Day in, day out, he lay in his bed and he slept. And the strange thing was that anyone who sat and watched over him at night disappeared and was never seen again. So the time came when there was no one left brave enough to sit with the prince at night.

When Kate heard about this, she said, "I'll do that. For a bag full of silver, I'll sit with the prince."

And the king agreed.

So that night Kate sat with the sleeping prince. All went well until midnight came. But as soon as the castle clock struck twelve, the prince rose from his bed as if in a daze, dressed himself and opened the door. Then off he went down the stairs, out the front door and into the stable, with Kate following at his heels. He saddled his horse, called his hound, and jumped into his saddle. And Kate leapt lightly up behind him.

Away they rode with the hound running alongside. They came to a wood of close-growing hazel, and as they wound in and out amongst the trees Kate picked hazelnuts from the branches and filled

her apron pockets with them. They rode on until they came to a green hill, and then the prince called out, "Open, open, green hill, and let the young prince in with his horse and hound."

"And," added Kate, "his fair lady behind him."

A door opened in the hillside, and they passed in and entered a magnificent hall that was brightly lit and full of handsome people dancing to the liveliest, most toe-tapping music Kate had ever heard.

Now as soon as they were inside, Kate slipped off the horse and hid in the shadows near the door. Immediately some beautiful ladies surrounded the prince and led him off to the dance. The prince danced with each beautiful lady in turn. He danced and he danced. He did not rest for a moment.

Then Kate knew that she was in the hall of the fairy folk, and she knew too that she must be careful, for if they caught her spying on them they would never ever let her go. So she drew back and hid herself in the darkest shadows she could find.

After a while she happened to notice a fairy child playing with a silver wand, and then she heard one of the fairy women say, "You take care of that wand. Three strokes from it, just three, would make that poor wee lassie with the sheep's head as bonnie as ever she was!"

So Kate took some hazelnuts out of her pocket and rolled them towards the fairy child. She rolled them and she rolled them until the

child dropped the wand and chased after the nuts. And Kate crept forward, snatched up the wand, and hid it under her apron.

Then the cock crowed. The prince came and mounted his horse, and Kate leapt lightly up behind him, and they rode back to the castle with the hound running alongside.

When the horse was in the stable, and the prince once more asleep in his bed, Kate sat down by the fire and cracked some nuts and ate them.

In the morning the king, the queen and the prince's younger brother came to the room, and Kate told them that the prince had had a good night. That was all.

The king asked Kate to watch over his son for yet another night. "I'll do that," she said. "For a bag full of gold, I'll sit with the prince."

Now the moment they had all gone, Kate took the wand and hurried up to the attic room to find her sister. She touched her three times with the wand and, there and then, the sheep's head disappeared and her sister was as bonnie as ever she was!

The next night came, and the same things happened as before. When the clock struck twelve, the prince rose from his bed, dressed, went down the stairs and out the front door, saddled his horse and called his hound. He mounted and Kate leapt up behind him. They took the winding path through the woods and Kate picked hazelnuts and filled her apron pockets. They came to the green hill, and the prince said, "Open, open, green hill and let the young prince in with his horse and hound."

"And," added Kate, "his fair lady behind him."

The door swung open, and they entered the hall where the beautiful dancers danced and the fiddlers played. And again Kate hid in the shadows, while the prince danced without resting for a moment.

After a while Kate noticed a fairy child playing with a white bird, chasing it and catching it. Then she heard one of the fairy women say, "You take care of that bird. Three bites of it, just three, would set the prince free from our fairy enchantment and make him as well as ever he was."

So Kate took some hazelnuts out of her pocket and rolled them towards the child. She rolled them and she rolled them until the child let go of the bird and chased after them. And Kate crept forward, snatched up the bird and hid it under her apron.

Then the cock crowed, and the prince mounted his horse, and Kate leapt up behind him. And they were off, back to the palace, with the hound running alongside.

When the horse was in the stable, and the prince once more asleep in his bed, Kate killed the bird, plucked off its feathers, and hung it over the fire to roast. Before long a rich, savoury smell filled the room. And then the prince woke up.

"Oh!" he said. "I'd like a taste of that bird!" So Kate gave him a bite.

He rose up on his elbow and, by and by, he said, "Oh! I'd like another taste of that bird!" So Kate gave him a second bite.

He sat up in his bed and, by and by, he said, "Oh! if only I could have another taste of that bird!" So Kate gave him a third bite.

Then he leapt up from his bed, fit and well as ever he was. In the morning when the king, the queen and the younger brother came, they found Kate and the prince sitting by the fire, cracking nuts and eating them, and rattling on about this and that, like old friends.

The king *was* happy. He said to Kate, "I promised you a bag full of silver and a bag full of gold, and they shall be yours. But that is not enough, for you have done more than watch over my son. You have healed him. So ask for anything you wish."

"Anything?" asked Kate.

"Yes, anything that I have is yours," said the king.

"Then," said Kate, "what I'd like best of all is to marry the prince!"

There, she said it! Kate was not shy.

And the prince? What about him? He was more than willing. He was eager to marry this bright-eyed, lively Kate.

Not long after, the prince's younger brother said that he wanted to marry the other Kate, the bonnie sister who had been sick. So, in

the end, there was a double wedding. The two Kates married the two brothers.

So there they were again—two Kates in the same family. And it would have been confusing, but the prince who had been sick said that he was going to call his Kate *Kate Crackernuts*, because it was while they sat by the fire cracking hazelnuts that he had first come to know her and love her.

Scottish

· THE · KING · WHO · WANTED · TO · · TOUCH · THE · MOON ·

Long ago there lived a king who always had to have his own way. Everyone had to do exactly what he said. Immediately. No talk, no arguing.

Well, one night this king looked out of the window and saw the silvery moon riding high in the sky and, there and then, he wanted to reach out and touch it. But even he couldn't do that. So he thought about it, and he thought about it. Night and day he thought about it. And at last he worked out a way of touching the moon. He would have a tall, tall tower built that reached to the sky, and then, when he had climbed to the top, he would be able to touch the moon.

So the king sent for the royal carpenter and ordered him to build the tower.

The carpenter shook his head. "A tower so tall that it reaches

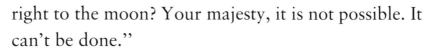

right to the moon? Your majesty, it is not possible. It can't be done."

"Can't!" shouted the king. "No such word as can't in this kingdom. Come back tomorrow morning, first thing, and tell me exactly how you are going to build my tower."

That night the carpenter did some hard thinking, and in the end he worked out a way of building a tall tower.

The next morning he went to the king and said, "Your majesty, the way to build the tower is to pile up lots of strong wooden chests, one on top of the other, hundreds and thousands of them, until they reach to the sky."

Now the king liked this idea. So he ordered his subjects to search their homes and bring all their strong chests to the palace. Immediately. And if anyone refused? Well, there was plenty of room in the royal prisons for them.

So, of course, the people brought their chests and gave them to the king. And there were all kinds of chests—big and small, carved, polished, painted and plain.

Then the carpenter and his assistant set to work. They laid chest upon chest, one on top of the other, up and up, and before long, outside the palace, there stood a tall tower. But when all the chests had been used, the tower did not even reach to the clouds.

The king said to the carpenter, "Make some more chests!"

So wood was found and the carpenter and his

assistants sawed and hammered and made more chests. Then they added these to the tower, laying chest upon chest, one on top of the other, up and up. But when all the chests had been used, the tower only reached to the clouds.

The king said to the carpenter, "Make some more chests!"

"There is no more wood, your majesty," said the carpenter.

"Then cut down all the trees and get some wood," ordered the king.

The carpenter shook his head. "*All* the trees!" he said. "Oh no, we can't do that—"

"Did I hear you say 'can't'? Have you forgotten that there is no such word as can't in this kingdom?" said the king. "Go and cut down *all* the trees. Immediately."

So then all the trees in the kingdom were chopped down—the great ancient trees and the slender saplings, the fruit trees and the nut trees and the flowering trees—all were cut down and sawn into planks and made into chests. More and more chests. And the chests were laid one on top of the other. Up and up. And when all the chests had been used, the tower reached beyond the clouds and up into the sky.

The king looked at the tower and he was pleased. He said, "The time has come for me to climb my tall, tall tower and touch the moon."

He began to climb, up and up and up, until at last he stood at the top of his tall, tall tower. He looked up and he stretched out both his arms, but he could not quite reach to the moon. He stood on the very tips of his toes and stretched some more. He was so very close. He could almost touch the moon. But not quite.

He shouted down, "Bring up another chest! Just one! That will be enough!"

The carpenter looked around. There were no chests left. No wood left. And not a single tree in all the land.

So he called out, "Your majesty, there are *no more chests*!"

The king shouted back, "THEN TAKE ONE OUT FROM THE BOTTOM AND BRING THAT UP HERE."

The carpenter was astonished. He couldn't take a chest out from the bottom of the pile. Well, could he? Surely, the king was not serious. Then he heard the king shouting again.

"DIDN'T YOU HEAR ME? TAKE ONE OUT FROM THE BOTTOM! IMMEDIATELY!"

The carpenter raised his eyebrows, shrugged his shoulders and then did as he was told. He pulled a chest out from the bottom of the pile.

And you can imagine what happened next. The whole tall tower came tumbling down, king, chests and all. So that was the end of the king who always had to have his own way and who wanted, above everything else, to touch the moon.

Caribbean

· THREE · GOLDEN · APPLES ·

Once there was a happy king. He had a large kingdom, a lovely queen and a daughter, Princess Isabelle, who was as beautiful as the day.

But misfortune creeps up from behind, and one night Princess Isabelle fell ill. A great troop of doctors came to the palace to examine her. They stroked their beards and they shook their heads. They had no idea what was the matter, so they tried first one medicine and then another. But nothing helped the princess, and as time passed, she began to fade away, until it seemed she would die.

Now what could the king do? He was willing to see anyone and try anything, if only he could save his daughter.

Well, one morning an old man came to the palace and he said to the king, "You must find the golden apples!"

"Golden apples!" exclaimed the king. "What golden apples?"

"In a far distant corner of the kingdom," said the old man, "there is a garden where wild nightingales sing, night and day, and in the garden stands an apple tree, all white with blossom, and on the tree hang nine golden apples. Three of these apples will cure your daughter."

Here was good news at last! The king straightaway ordered his heralds to go and proclaim in every town and village that the man who brought the golden apples and cured the Princess Isabelle would be richly rewarded. He could even marry the princess and inherit the kingdom!

Now, in a distant corner of the land, there lived a poor peasant and his three sons. All they had was a small house, a cow, some hens and a garden. But in that garden wild nightingales sang, night and day, and there grew an apple tree, all white with blossom, and on the tree hung nine golden apples.

As soon as the three brothers heard the king's proclamation, they all wanted to take the apples and try their luck. But the eldest insisted that, as he was the eldest, he must go first. So he picked the three biggest apples, put them in a basket, covered them with a clean cloth, and off he went.

He had not gone far, when he met an old woman. "What's in your basket, my friend?" she asked.

"Slimy toads!" he answered rudely. "Just slimy toads!"

"And slimy toads they shall be!" she said.

The eldest brother walked and he walked until he reached the palace. And when he told the guards that he had brought three golden apples, he was taken straight through the corridors and up the steps to where the king and queen sat on their royal thrones.

"Your majesties," said the lad, "I have brought you three golden apples."

The king smiled. He lifted the cloth and put his hand in the basket and—oh! what was this? *Three slimy toads!*

The king jumped to his feet and gave the lad a hard slap that sent him rolling down the steps—toads, basket and all!

So the eldest brother trudged home and told his family about his bad luck. Golden apples that changed into toads!

The second brother was sure he could do better. So he picked the next three biggest apples, put them in a basket, covered them with a clean cloth, and off he went.

He had not gone far, when he met the same old woman. "What's in your basket, my friend?" she said.

"Slithery snakes!" he answered rudely. "Just slithery snakes!"

"And slithery snakes they shall be!" she said.

The second brother walked and walked until he reached the palace. Then he, too, was taken straight through the corridors and up the steps to where the king and queen sat on their thrones.

"Your majesties," said the second brother, "I have brought you three golden apples."

The king smiled. He lifted the cloth and put his hand in the basket and—oh! what was this? *Three slithery snakes!*

Up jumped the king, and he gave this lad *two* hard slaps that sent him rolling, twice as fast, down the steps—snakes, basket and all!

So the second brother trudged home and told his family about his bad luck. Golden apples that changed into snakes!

Then the youngest brother, who was called Martin, said that it was now his turn to go.

"You—the youngest and smallest!" laughed the eldest brother.

"You think you can do better than us!" scoffed the second.

"I can try," said Martin.

So he picked the three remaining apples from the tree, put them in a basket and covered them with a clean cloth. Then, with clean clogs on his feet and best clothes on his back, he was on his way, whistling like a blackbird in spring.

He had not gone far, when he met the same old woman. "What's in your basket, my friend?" she said.

63

"Three golden apples, madame," he answered. "Just three golden apples."

"And three golden apples they shall be," she said. "But, tell me, what are these apples for?"

"These apples will cure Princess Isabelle," said Martin. "And then, of course, I shall marry her."

"Marry a princess? Ah—you may need extra help for that," said the old woman. "So take this silver whistle. It could be useful."

Martin thanked her and dropped the whistle in his pocket.

Then he walked and he walked, and when he reached the palace, like his two brothers before him, he was taken straight to the king and queen.

He bowed. "Your majesties," he said, "I have brought you three golden apples."

The king frowned. He was suspicious. And no wonder! He lifted the cloth, very slowly, very carefully, and peered into the basket.

"Three golden apples!" he exclaimed.

The king seized the basket and then he was off—striding along to Princess Isabelle's room, with the queen at his heels, and Martin and a crowd of royal courtiers behind.

Princess Isabelle ate one golden apple and she sighed. She ate a second and she sat up in bed. She ate a third and she jumped out of bed, well and happy and more beautiful than ever.

She said, "Now I must marry the lad who brought the golden apples."

Martin looked at Princess Isabelle. Yes, he liked the idea of marrying her. She was pretty, very pretty.

But the king looked at his daughter and he thought, "A princess is a princess. But a peasant . . . *hmmm* . . . a peasant is only a peasant. So we shall see."

He said to Martin, "You will have to prove yourself, before you can marry my daughter. The princess has one hundred pet hares

which are kept in my stables. Tomorrow you must take those hares out to graze in the fields and bring them back, in the evening—every single one of them."

"It sounds hard," said Martin. "But I can try."

Next morning the king's servants opened the stable doors, and by the time the last hare came leaping out, the first one was out of sight.

"Impossible to find them again!" thought Martin, slouching along with his hands in his pockets. And then he touched the whistle. Could it be useful? He took it out and blew a long blast.

Hares came bounding towards him from all sides. He counted them. There were one hundred exactly! His troubles were over. He led the hares out to a big meadow and let them play there, while he lay in the grass and thought about this and that. When evening came, he blew the whistle and—*forward march!*—off he went with the hares leaping along behind him.

The king could not believe his eyes when he saw them coming. He counted the hares. There were one hundred exactly.

"Humph!" he growled. "Before you can marry my daughter, you must look after the hares for a second day."

Next morning the stable doors were opened, and Martin again set off with the hares.

But the king was crafty, and he had made some plans. In the afternoon a woman came riding along on a donkey. She was

wearing an old, faded dress, and had a scarf tied round her head and clogs on her feet. She looked like a poor peasant. But Martin was not fooled. He knew it was the queen. He recognised the face.

"Please sell me one of your hares," she said. "It would make such a good dinner for my hungry little children."

"The hares are not for sale," said Martin. "But you can earn one."

"And what must I do?"

"Give me three rosy kisses!" he replied. "That is all you have to do!"

This was not the sort of thing to ask of a queen. But she wanted one of those hares, so she gave him three quick kisses.

Martin then picked up a hare and gave it to her, and she rode off, holding it tightly in her arms. But before she reached the palace gates, he blew the whistle, and the hare wriggled free and came bounding back to him.

In the evening, Martin again blew his whistle and—*forward march!*—back to the palace he went with the hares leaping along behind him.

The king did some more careful counting, and he found that there were one hundred hares exactly. But he was not going to be beaten.

"Humph!" he growled. "Before you can marry my daughter, you must look after the hares for a third day."

Next morning Martin went off with the hares yet again. But the king had made some more plans, and in the afternoon a man came along riding on a donkey. He was wearing a patched jacket, torn trousers, a black beret on his head and clogs on his feet. He looked like a poor peasant, but Martin recognised the face immediately. It was the king himself.

"Sell me one of your hares," he said. "I'll give you a good price."

"The hares are not for sale," said Martin. "But you can earn one."

"And what must I do?"

"Well," said Martin, "I shall cut a branch off this wild rose bush. Then you must bend over, and I will give you three whacks!"

68

This was *definitely* not the sort of thing to ask of a king. But he did want one of those hares. So he climbed down from the donkey and bent over, and Martin gave him three whacks—one, two, three.

Then the king mounted the donkey, and Martin handed him a hare. The king held that hare very tightly as he rode off. But before he could reach the palace gates, Martin blew the whistle, and the hare wriggled free and came bounding back to him.

Evening came, the whistle was blown again and—*forward march!* —back to the palace went Martin with the hares leaping along behind him.

And when the king did his counting, all the hares were there.

"Humph!" he growled. "Come to the palace tomorrow morning!"

Next morning there was Martin at the palace. The king and the queen and Princess Isabelle sat on their royal thrones, and the courtiers were gathered below them. Martin thought that now, at last, he had won the princess. But no!

The king said, "Before you can marry my daughter, you must prove that you have wit and wisdom. You must talk and keep on talking, until you have told me a whole sack full of interesting truths. And only when *I* say that the sack is full, can you stop talking and marry her."

Martin grinned. He could think of some very good truths that would help fill that sack.

"Here is the first truth," he began. "One day when I was guarding Princess Isabelle's pet hares, the queen came along. She was dressed like a peasant and sitting on a donkey. And, would you believe it, she wanted a hare. She wanted it so much that she gave me . . ."

"No!" cried the king. "No! no! no! I won't listen!"

"The queen gave me three kisses for one hare!"

There. The king couldn't say that was a lie.

"Now the next day, when I was guarding the hares," said Martin, "the king came along. He was dressed like a peasant and sitting on a donkey. And, would you believe it, he too wanted a hare . . ."

"Oh! Don't tell!" cried the king.

"And he wanted it so much that he . . ."

"That's enough!"

"His Royal Majesty bent . . ."

"Stop! stop!"

"He bent over and I . . ."

"Stop! You have said enough! The sack is full! Completely full! You can marry my daughter!"

And so the next day Martin married Princess Isabelle, and very happy she was too, for she loved him, even though he was a peasant lad and she was a princess.

French

70

· THE · MAGIC · FRUIT ·

In the time, long ago, when great and marvellous magicians lived on earth, Coniraya was the greatest. With his hollow stick he could flatten mountains. He could bring water to dry places. He could make magic that was big and strong. Yet, sometimes, because he liked jokes and pranks, he just looked around and made mischief.

Now while Coniraya was the greatest among magicians, there was a young woman called Cavillaca who was the most beautiful. She was so beautiful that every young man, as soon as he saw her, wanted to marry her. But Cavillaca was proud; no living man was handsome enough or powerful enough for her. And so she refused to marry.

One day Coniraya was walking about the world disguised as a poor Indian, when he saw Cavillaca sitting under a tree, weaving. Then, like every other young man, he wanted to marry her.

71

"Greetings, beautiful Cavillaca," he said.

But Cavillaca kept her eyes on her weaving.

So Coniraya thought up some mischief. Next moment—there he was—a large bird with glorious rainbow-coloured feathers. He spread his wide wings and flew up to sit on a branch of the lucuma tree that stretched out above Cavillaca, and he began to sing.

But still she kept her eyes on the weaving.

Then Coniraya thought up some more mischief. He conjured up a fruit. A lovely ripe golden-orange fruit. And he hid strong magic inside that fruit and dropped it straight down into Cavillaca's lap.

Well, the fruit looked so lovely, she had to pick it up. Then it smelt so good, she had to bite into it. And the taste was so delicious, she ate it to the last juicy mouthful.

She did not guess that it was a magic fruit.

Months passed by, and because of the magic fruit, Cavillaca had a son. He was a happy, smiling, beautiful baby, and she loved him with a great love.

But she was curious and kept wondering who had made the magic and given her this baby . . . and how it had been done . . . and when.

She thought about it and thought about it; and when the baby was almost a year old and could crawl, she decided that she would find out who was the father of her beautiful child, and then she would marry him, because, without doubt, he must be both exceedingly powerful and exceedingly handsome. So she summoned the great magicians to a meeting.

Of course, all the magicians came dressed in their most splendid robes, hoping that Cavillaca would notice them. All except for Coniraya, who was dressed, once again, in the torn, shabby clothes of a poor Indian.

The meeting began, and Cavillaca stood, proud and beautiful, with her baby in her arms. "Until this time I have always refused to marry," she said, "but now I solemnly promise that I will marry the father of my son, if he will make himself known to me."

But no one spoke. No one moved.

"If you will not speak, then my son shall tell me," said Cavillaca. "He will know his father and go to him." And she put the baby on the ground.

Immediately, he was off, crawling eagerly straight towards the shabby Indian. And when he reached the Indian's feet, he looked up and stretched out his arms.

Proud Cavillaca was angry.

"A poor Indian! No, I will *not* marry a poor Indian!" she cried as she ran to the baby and swept him up in her arms. "Though I have given my promise," she said, "I will *never* marry him. I would rather die . . ."

And she clasped the baby close to her and ran off.

"Stop!" Coniraya called out. "Stop! Things are not as they seem!"

But Cavillaca ran on and would not listen.

Then Coniraya struck the ground with his hollow stick. Next moment—there he was dressed in magnificent robes, dazzling and golden.

He called, "Beautiful Cavillaca, look back! Turn your eyes towards me and see how handsome and splendid I have become!"

But she ran on.

And Coniraya was afraid of her stubborn pride and sorry for his own mischief-making, and he ran after her. But she heard him coming and gathered together her own powerful magic and hid herself from him and ran faster, faster, ever faster.

Though he could not tell where Cavillaca had gone, Coniraya was determined to find her. He ran and ran, asking everyone he met if they had seen her, but no one had. At last, good fortune came, and he met the Condor who had seen her and was able to show him the way.

Coniraya blessed the Condor. "I give you power to fly over the valleys and wild places, and to eat where you will," he said. "A curse be on those who kill the Condor."

Coniraya ran on and more good fortune came. He met the Falcon who had also seen Cavillaca and was able to show him the way.

Coniraya blessed the Falcon. "I give you power to soar above the mountains," he said. "In song and dance the Indian shall always praise the Falcon."

Coniraya ran on and again good fortune came. He met the Puma who was also able to show him the way.

Coniraya blessed the Puma. "I give you power over all other living creatures," he said. "At all times and everywhere the Indian shall honour the Puma."

Coniraya ran on. He came to the sea and there he saw Cavillaca running across the sandy shore. He called to her, but she would not look back.

She gathered together her magic powers, and, holding the baby close in her arms, she plunged into the sea. Next moment—there was no beautiful Cavillaca and no baby. They were gone.

In their place stood two rocks, a large one and a small one close beside it. Two rocks and the waves gently lapping against them. That was all.

Peruvian

75

·SEVEN·CLEVER·BROTHERS·

Once upon a time there lived a king and a queen who had seven sons, each one born on a different day of the week, from Sunday through to Saturday; and they named each son after the day he was born. The eldest was called Sunday, the next Monday and so on, through to the youngest who was called Saturday. And when those princes grew up, they were all clever, all handsome and, all seven of them, good friends.

Now one day the brothers decided the time had come for them to leave home and see the world. But when they told the king, he said, "You can all go except for Saturday. I must keep one of my sons with me, and he is the youngest and smallest."

But Saturday did not want to be left behind and kept on asking. He wouldn't keep quiet. And in the end the king said that he could go.

"Only promise me one thing," said the king, "that, whatever

happens, you will never quarrel, but always stay friends as brothers should." And the brothers promised. They could think of no reason why they should ever want to quarrel.

So, next day, they set off. They walked and walked, for seven days under a hot sun they walked, until they came to a place where seven roads lay before them. Then each brother wanted to choose a different road.

Sunday, the eldest, said, "Let us each take our own road, go our separate ways and then meet here again one year from today."

Then each one strode off down his own road, and exactly one year later, they all met again at the same place. And immediately they began talking, the way brothers do.

Saturday, the youngest, said to the eldest, "Well, Sunday, what's the news? What did you find in the big world?"

"Oh! I found something marvellous!" said Sunday. "A pair of spectacles!"

"Nothing marvellous about that," said Saturday.

"Isn't there now? Well, if you put these spectacles on your nose, little brother, you can see anything that's happening up to five hundred miles away."

"Now that is something!" said Monday, and his brothers nodded their heads. "But—guess what? I also found something marvellous. An old fiddle!"

Saturday shrugged his shoulders, "Is that all?" he asked.

"Ah—but if strangers hear me play this fiddle, it sends them to sleep."

"That could be useful," said Tuesday. "Now—don't laugh—and I'll tell you what I've learnt. I can take things out of anyone's pocket, even out of their hands, so lightly they don't notice."

"So you're a pickpocket! Amazing!" said Wednesday. "But I think I too can surprise you. I found a coat. And this coat has a pocket. And I can put anything into this pocket. Doesn't matter how big. It will always fit."

"That's something to be proud of!" said Thursday. "All I have is a little twig from an oak tree. *But*, if I swish it to and fro, it will send big, thick oak cudgels flying through the air to beat my enemies. One or a hundred. It can manage anything!"

"That could be useful in wartime," said Friday. "As for me, I've learnt to shoot with a bow and arrow. I can hit anything. Even a seed in a bird's beak, miles away!"

"So, you're a crack shot!" said Saturday. "Me, I've learnt to do some throwing and catching. I can throw anything with my right hand, even a heavy millstone, high as I like and then catch it in my left hand."

"Show us, little brother!" said Sunday. "Show us!"

"You will have to wait and see," said Saturday.

Then, after a lot more talking, the brothers decided that they would travel together for a while before returning home. So they drew lots to decide which road to take, and off they went.

They walked and they walked and that evening they came to a strange and silent city, all draped in black, where everyone looked sad. It seemed that the king's only daughter had vanished, and no one knew where she was or who had taken her.

When the brothers heard this, they looked at each other and they all thought the same thing. Perhaps *they* could find the princess. So they went to the king and offered to find her.

The king said, "The one who finds my daughter can have half my kingdom, half my treasure *and* marry my daughter, if she is willing."

Then Sunday went to the window, put his spectacles on his nose and looked. "I can see a dark and dismal castle," he said. "And in it an old man—face the colour of parchment, long grey hair and robes of black and gold. And next to him stands a beautiful maiden, and her eyes are filled with tears."

"Tell me," said the king. "What does she look like?"

"On her left hand she has six fingers," said Sunday.

"Then she is indeed my daughter," said the king. "And the old man is the sorceror who wanted to marry her. Alas, you will not be able to save her, for he is a clever, wily magician."

"Trust us," said Sunday. "We shall find her and bring her back."

Then the seven brothers set off, with Sunday showing them the way to go. They walked and walked, until at last they came to the dark and dismal castle. They gave seven loud knocks at the door and told the servant who opened it that they were seven princes who had come to see the sorceror.

"He is busy celebrating his marriage," said the servant.

"Then we are only just in time," said Monday. "We have come to play music at the wedding feast."

So the brothers were taken to a splendid hall; and there, surrounded by wedding guests, stood the sorceror, and beside him a sad-faced maiden whom he held firmly by the hand.

And then . . . well, *then* Monday tucked his fiddle under his chin and played soft, sleepy music, and everyone, except for the brothers themselves, closed their eyes and fell asleep. Then Tuesday crept across the room, released the princess from the sorceror's grasp and gave her to Wednesday. And Wednesday slipped her into his coat pocket—and she fitted inside it perfectly.

Then the brothers hurried off. They passed the servants in the corridors and the guards outside. No one stopped them. No one guessed that they had taken the princess.

But when the sorceror woke up, he knew immediately what had happened, and he ordered a company of soldiers to ride out and capture the princess and the seven princes.

Now the brothers had not gone far along the road when they heard the sound of horses' hooves. They looked back and saw the soldiers galloping towards them. So Thursday took out his little twig and swished it to and fro. The next moment hundreds of oak cudgels came flying through the air and beat those soldiers till they were so frightened they turned right round and rode back to the castle.

The brothers walked and walked, for three hours under a hot sun they walked, until they were so tired they had to sit down under a tree and rest. Then Wednesday took the princess out of his pocket.

She soon woke up and opened her eyes and—*well!*—she was more than a little surprised to see where she was. But when the brothers told her who they were and how they had saved her she was so grateful that she thanked them over and over again. Then they all talked together some more, until, one after the other, they fell asleep.

Now when the soldiers returned to the castle and told the sorceror about the oak cudgels, he realised that capturing the princess was work he must do himself. He shivered all over . . . and changed into a great black bird. Then he spread his wings and flew up into the sky. He looked north and south. He looked east and west. And he

saw the brothers and the princess asleep under a tree. He swooped down, seized the princess and off he flew.

She called out, as loud as she could, and the brothers woke up and saw the bird high in the sky, with the princess in his beak.

Friday jumped to his feet, grabbed his bow, and aimed an arrow at the bird's eye. And, sure enough, he hit it.

The bird let go of the princess and she fell down . . . down . . . down . . . towards the earth. But Saturday was ready: he stretched out his left arm, opened his hand and caught her. She was safe!

Then the princess and the seven brothers all set off together, taking the road back to her father's palace. But on the way the brothers, those seven brothers who had always been friends, started to quarrel. The princess was so beautiful that they *all* wanted to marry her.

Sunday said, "If I hadn't looked through my spectacles, we wouldn't have found out where she was. So she should be mine."

"Yes," said Monday, "but if I hadn't played my fiddle and sent everyone to sleep, we wouldn't have been able to rescue her."

"But who was the one who took her out of the sorceror's hand so carefully that no one woke?" asked Tuesday.

"If I hadn't hidden her in my coat, the guards would have seen her as we left," said Wednesday. "So she surely belongs to me."

"All quite true," said Thursday, "but if I had not used my little twig and beaten the soldiers, they would have captured her again."

"But," said Friday, "if I hadn't shot at the great black bird and killed him, what then?"

"You have all had your say," said Saturday. "So now be good enough to listen to me. If I had not caught the princess as she fell from the sky, she would have died. But still . . . we are all big fools for quarrelling. We promised our father that we would always stay friends. And besides, what about the princess? What does she think? Maybe she won't want to marry any of us!"

Saturday turned to the princess who was walking along behind them. There was a smile on her face. She had been listening and had heard every word!

"Without the help of all seven of you," she said, "I would not be standing here. But my choice is made. I wish to marry Saturday, the youngest and smallest, because when I was falling helpless from the sky and most afraid, he caught me and held me safe. Without Saturday, I would have died."

So that was settled.

Now when they came at last to the palace, the king welcomed them with open arms and the celebrations began. Trumpets sounded, cannons boomed and flags flew from every tower and steeple.

A few days later, there was a great and glorious wedding when Saturday married the princess. And then there were *more* celebrations!

After the wedding, the king offered the seven brothers half of all that he had—his kingdom and his treasures—as a reward for finding and saving his daughter. But Saturday said that everything should be given to his brothers. He had been rewarded enough already. He had married the princess. So the six brothers shared everything between them. And there were no quarrels. Not even a small disagreement.

Then the seven princes, and the princess with them, returned to their own kingdom, and—*well!*—the king, their father, was so happy and proud when he saw them and heard their news.

"My sons," he said, "you are clever, handsome young men and besides that good friends. So, for what more can I ask? Only one thing. A daughter. And now you have brought me one, the beautiful princess, wife of my youngest son, Saturday!"

And then the celebrations began all over again!

Jewish

84

· THE · PRINCE · AND · THE · · FLYING · CARPET ·

There was once a prince who was so fond of hunting that he rode out every day in search of game. But one day he had no luck and by late afternoon had caught nothing. He rode on and on until he reached a dark jungle where he had never been before. There he came upon a flock of parrots, perched in amongst the trees, and he lifted his bow and took aim.

But before he could shoot, there was a whirl and flurry of feathers and the parrots flew up and away, leaving one bird still sitting there.

"Do not shoot me!" said the bird. "I am the raja of all parrots. I am the one that can tell you about Princess Maya."

The prince lowered his bow and rode up to the bird. "Princess Maya!" he said. "Who is Princess Maya?"

"Ahhh—the beautiful Princess Maya," said the parrot. "What can I say? She is radiant as the moon . . . warm and gentle as the evening sun. In this great world she is beyond compare."

"Where does she live?" asked the prince. "And how can I find her?"

"Go forward, ever forward," said the parrot, "through dark jungles and across wide plains, and you will find her."

Then the prince rode home and on the way he made up his mind to find the beautiful Princess Maya, even if he had to search the whole world.

When he told his mother and father about the beautiful princess, they were sad. He was their only child, their golden treasure, and they did not want to lose him. But the prince had decided to go and he would not change his mind.

The very next morning he dressed in his finest clothes, took his bow and arrows and some food for the journey, mounted his favourite horse and set off.

Well, he rode until he reached the dark jungle where he had seen the parrots. And then he rode forward, ever forward. He crossed a wide plain, and still he rode forward. He entered a second, even darker jungle and, all of a sudden, he heard loud, angry voices; and in a clearing near by, he saw three demons—three small, sharp-eyed, wicked-looking demons—bunched round a small pile of things lying on the ground. There was a bag, a stick and an ancient carpet.

"What is the matter?" asked the prince.

One of the demons pointed to the things lying on the ground, "Our master died and left us these," he said, "and I want *all* of them!"

"And so do I!" shouted the second demon.

"Me too!" shrieked the third.

"A bag, a stick and an old carpet?" said the prince. "They're not worth quarrelling about!"

"Not worth quarrelling about!" The first demon squalled it out, fair cracked his throat. "Not worth quarrelling about! Why, the bag will give you anything you ask for. And the stick will beat your enemies and—see the rope coiled round it?—that will tie them up so they can't escape. As for the carpet . . . it will take you anywhere you want to go."

"Is that so?" said the prince. And he did some quick thinking. "Maybe I could help settle the quarrel," he suggested. "I shall take three arrows and shoot them in the air, and the first one of you to find an arrow and bring it back can have all the treasures."

"Yes! yes!" the little demons agreed. Each one certain *he* was the fastest runner. Each one certain *he* would win.

So the prince let fly three arrows, and off they ran, full pelt.

And what next? The prince jumped down from his horse, turned it round to face the way they had come and said, "Lift your hooves, my fine horse, and gallop home!" And the horse galloped off.

The prince picked up the stick and the bag. He unrolled the carpet, sat down on it, crossed his legs and said, "Carpet! Take me to the city where Princess Maya lives!"

The carpet fluttered and then rose slowly upwards. When it was higher than the trees, it simply flew through the air. Smooth and steady, it flew and it flew, over dark jungles and wide plains. It flew and it flew, until it came to the edge of a great city. Then it gently floated downwards.

As soon as the carpet touched the ground, the prince stood up, stretched himself and looked around. He rolled up the carpet and, with the bag over his shoulder, the carpet tucked under his arm and the stick in his hand, he strode off into the city.

The first person he met was an old woman. "Is this the city where Princess Maya lives?" he asked.

"Indeed it is," she said.

"And how can I find her?" he asked.

"Every evening," said the old woman, "the princess comes and sits upon the palace roof for one whole hour, and—*oh! such great wonder!*—she lights the city with her beauty."

So that evening the prince waited outside the palace, and at sunset a slender maiden came and sat upon the roof. She wore a sari of shimmering silk and on her forehead was a golden band, set with diamonds and pearls. It seemed as if a silvery radiance shone around her: in her presence night became day.

The prince gazed upon the beautiful Princess Maya. He could not take his eyes off her. She truly was beyond compare.

At midnight, he held his bag and he said, "Bag! Give me a shawl of shimmering silk, the very match of Princess Maya's sari!" And there—inside the bag—was a shawl of shimmering silk.

He unrolled his carpet, sat down, crossed his legs and said, "Carpet! Take me to Princess Maya!"

The carpet rose up until it was higher than the roofs and flew over the city until it reached the palace. Then it went straight through an open window and landed in Princess Maya's room.

The prince looked around and saw the beautiful princess, lying asleep in her bed.

Soft and silent as a cat, he stood up and gently placed the silk shawl beside the sleeping princess. And then—back on the carpet—and he was off!

The next evening the prince again stood outside the palace and gazed upon the beautiful princess; and at midnight he said, "Bag! Give me a necklace of diamonds and pearls, the very match of Princess Maya's golden headband!" And there it was—a golden necklace set with diamonds and pearls.

Again he unrolled his carpet, sat down, crossed his legs and said, "Carpet! Take me to Princess Maya!" And again off he flew, right into her room. And this time he placed the necklace beside the sleeping princess. Then—back on the carpet—and he was off!

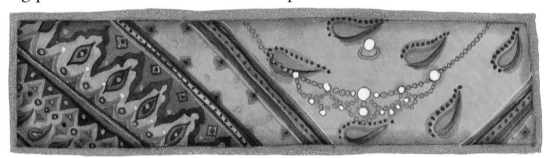

On the third evening the same things happened. The prince stood outside and gazed upon the beautiful princess; and at midnight he said, "Bag! Give me a golden ring set with the finest diamonds in the world!" And there it was—a splendid glittering ring.

Again he unrolled his carpet, sat down, crossed his legs and flew to the palace and into her room.

But this time he did not place the gift beside the sleeping princess. Instead he lifted her hand and slipped the ring on one of her fingers.

Princess Maya stirred and opened her eyes. And when she saw the handsome young prince who held her hand, she said, "So, you are the one who gave me the shawl and the necklace and now this ring.

Tell me, is there something you want, something I can give you in return?"

"There is," said the prince. "You yourself are the gift I seek, for you are the one I wish to marry."

Princess Maya was surprised by the prince's words, but after they had talked together for much of the night she agreed to marry this handsome, generous young man. And in the morning she took him to her father, the raja of that land, and asked for his consent to their marriage.

But the raja said, "This man is a stranger. One who came like a thief in the night. You cannot marry him."

The princess pleaded with her father until at last he agreed that if the prince could prove that he was a man of courage and strength then she could marry him.

The raja said to the prince, "Outside the city there lives a fearsome ogre. He is as tall as two, as broad as three and has the strength of six. My people live in fear of him. Day in, day out, he comes and kills and steals. If you can capture this ogre, then you may marry my daughter."

The prince thought to himself, "Capture an ogre? *This* is a task I can surely do!" And he set off with the stick in his hand.

He had not gone far when the mighty ogre saw him and came bounding towards him, roaring and bellowing in a great fury.

Then the prince said, "Stick! Do your work!" And the stick went flying through the air, and it beat the ogre until he fell helpless to the ground.

The prince said, "Rope! Do your work!" And the rope twirled itself off the stick and, quick as lightning, coiled itself round the ogre until he was bound, head to toe, so tight that he couldn't even move his little finger.

What then could the raja say? He had to agree to the marriage of the prince and his beautiful daughter, Princess Maya. So there was a wedding. And such a wedding! For a whole week there was feasting and rejoicing throughout the land.

At last the time came for the prince to return to his own land with his new bride. Then there was a long and magnificent procession:

the prince and princess and their attendants led the way, riding splendid black horses, and behind them trooped a hundred camels, bells jingling, all laden with treasures the raja had heaped upon them.

Now when the prince's horse had returned to the royal stables without a rider, his mother and father had been certain that their son was dead. So—imagine their happiness when he returned with his beautiful bride!

Well, the years passed, and the prince and beautiful Princess Maya lived together, happy and content. The prince always kept the bag, the stick and the carpet with him. And while the bag and the carpet were often useful, because his was a peaceful country and he had no enemies, he never again needed to use the stick.

Indian

· THE · HALLOWEEN · WITCHES ·

One Halloween night, when the moon didn't shine and the wild wind howled, a whole lot of old witches got together in a little wood cabin down in a hollow, behind the dark pines. A big supper was cooking on the stove, while they sat round the fire, telling mean tales and big lies about their friends and neighbours and talking about the spells they were going to conjure up soon as midnight came along.

By and by, a stranger, one who went about the world doing good, happened to come upon the wood cabin behind the dark pines; and he knocked at the door.

The witches called out, "Who's there? Who-oo? Who-oo?"

And a voice said, "A stranger. One who is hungry and cold."

Then they all laughed and sang out, "We're a-cookin' for ourselves! We'll not cook for you!"

The voice didn't say anything. But the knocking kept on, steady and soft.

The old witches took no notice. They emptied the frying pan, reached for the fresh-baked bread, and they began to eat. And, my goodness, how they did eat! eat! eat!

Same time, the knocking kept on, steady and soft, until, by and by, one of the witches called out, "Who's that a-knockin'? Who-oo? Who-oo?"

Then there came a sort of whistling, wailing sound:

"Let me in, do-oo!
I'm cold through and thro-oo-ugh
And I'm hungry to-oo!"

The witches laughed again and sang out, "Go away do! We're a-cookin' for ourselves! We'll not cook for you!"

Then they shuffled up closer to the fire and did some more eating. Same time the knocking kept on, steady and soft, until, by and by, the witches began to feel uneasy.

One of them said, "Let's give the stranger something and get him to go away before he spoils our spells when midnight comes along."

And she took a little, little, *little* piece of dough, about as big as a pea, and put it in the frying pan and set it on the stove. But soon as she put the dough on the pan it began to swell. It swelled over the pan. It swelled over the stove. It plumped down on the floor and, swift and strong, it swelled and rolled into every corner of the room.

The old witches got scared, and they ran to the door. *But the door was tight shut.*

So they hitched up their skirts and jumped up on the chair seats and perched there, arms akimbo. And still the dough swelled and rolled, and rose up and up, until it came over the seats of the chairs.

So then they climbed on the backs of the chairs and scrooged up small as they could while their eyes got bigger and rounder with

scaredness. And still the dough swelled and rolled, and same time the knocking kept on, steady and soft.

Then they called out again, "Who's that a-knockin'? Who-oo? Who-oo?"

The knocking stopped, and they heard these words creeping through every crack and cranny of the house:

"You refuse to give, you refuse to lend;
Criticise your neighbour, criticise your friend.
Now hush your tattling, hush your talk;
You'll never more have strength to walk!"

There and then, the witches' legs began to shrink until they were so small and weak, they could scarcely hop. They looked at each other and they were so surprised they blinked their eyes and turned their heads right round, front to back. They were no longer witches. They were owls.

And *then* they heard these words creeping through the house:

"Because you wouldn't open your door,
You shan't live in a house no more.
So fly out any window you see,
And live your life in a hollow tree!"

Well, by this time, the dough had risen so high that there was only a little gap left at the top of an open window. So the owls spread their wings and flew towards it, pushing and jostling, each one scared she wouldn't get out. But, one after the other, they managed somehow to fly out of that window and off into the woods, still calling out, "Who's that a-knockin'? Who-oo? Who-oo?"

And even to this day, in the dark of the night, those owls still fly about calling, always calling, "Who-oo? Who-oo?"

Except at Halloween. On that one night those owls turn back into witches and they sneak about the woods, weaving and conjuring up all their wicked and most mischievous spells.

Black American

·Koala·

Koala was a boy who lived long ago, in the dreamtime. He hadn't a mother or a father. He hadn't any brothers or sisters. He was alone in the tribe. And because of this he did exactly what he wanted and didn't listen to anyone. He pleased himself, and that meant he did no work *and* he got up to lots of mischief of one kind or another.

Now one year, when the dry time came, all the streams and rivers and billabongs dried up, and the people had to walk a long way to the waterholes in order to get enough to drink. Everyone who was big and strong enough went and fetched some water, except for Koala. He didn't like to go walking. So he stayed behind in the camp, making mischief. And when the others came back, he went round begging for a drink, until someone took pity and gave him some water.

But a day came when no one would give Koala a drink. Everyone said he should pick up his own wooden coolamon and go and get his own water.

Next morning the men went hunting, the women and children went off to dig for roots, and there was only one person left in the camp. Koala. And, by this time, he was feeling very thirsty. So he went round the camp looking for water. But he couldn't find any. All the precious water had been very carefully hidden.

He looked here . . . there . . . everywhere. He didn't give up. And in the end he found a whole lot of coolamons full of water, hidden in the bush under some shady trees.

So Koala had a great, long drink. And when he was full and couldn't drink another drop, he said, "I know what I'll do. I'll hide the water in my own secret place. Then I won't be thirsty again for a long time."

He took a full coolamon, climbed up a small gum tree and hid it on a branch, among the leaves. Then he fetched the rest of the coolamons, one after the other, and hid them in the tree.

He had just hidden the last one when the tree stirred itself, and— strong magic—it sprang up and up *and up*, until it became an enormous tree. Koala hung on tight, and when the tree stopped growing, he found himself near the top, with the coolamons around him. He thought he could climb down. But could he climb up again? He wasn't sure about that. So he sat down on a big branch, right up against the trunk, and had a little snooze.

At sunset, when everyone returned to the camp, they were so hot and thirsty they went straight to the hiding place to get a drink. But they soon found that there were only a few coolamons there; and they were empty.

Immediately, everyone had the same thought. "Koala! Where is Koala?"

And they looked around and saw an enormous tree where there had only been a small tree before, and near the top was Koala *and* all the coolamons!

"Koala!" they shouted. "Bring down our water!"

But Koala laughed. He felt safe at the top of that enormous tree. "If you want the water," he called out, "come and get it yourselves!"

Then a young man said, "I'll bring down the water. It is a very tall tree, but I can climb it!"

His friend said, "And I'll bring down that rascal Koala, so that we can deal with him!"

So they climbed the tree trunk while Koala peered down through the branches, watching them. When they had almost reached the top, Koala lifted a coolamon and poured water down the trunk and over the two young men. And then their hands slipped on the smooth wet bark, and they lost their grip and went sliding down to the bottom of the tree.

Then two brothers offered to climb the tree. But they didn't go straight up, hand over hand. They were cunning and swung them-

selves round and round the trunk, in a spiral. Koala waited until they had almost reached him, and then he poured water over them. But they swung themselves round the trunk so swiftly that the water missed them; and they climbed on and up, coming closer and closer. Then Koala was afraid, and he began to moan and wail and cry.

And next thing, one of the brothers reached out and grabbed him. Koala struggled hard and managed to break free. But then he lost his balance and fell, bouncing from branch to branch, right to the ground.

Every single bone in his body hurt. But Koala didn't wait. He jumped up and he ran. And everyone was so angry; they chased after him, shaking their fists and shouting. They were determined to catch him. And they almost did. But just in time he reached another tree, and he scurried up it, fast as he could.

And then, before their eyes—strong magic—Koala changed. Rough grey hair covered his body. His ears stood up, all fringed and furry, above two round black-button eyes and a small black shiny nose. He was no longer Koala the boy. He had become Koala the bear.

Even today, Koala looks exactly the same. And—would you believe it?—he still won't go looking for water if he can help it. When he is thirsty, he nibbles some more juicy leaves from a gum tree, and that's usually enough for him.

But he has not forgotten the day when he was in trouble and was nearly caught, for if anyone tries to climb his tree he always makes a great fuss and moans and wails and cries, just as he did when he was a little boy called Koala.

Australian

· Baba · Yaga · Bony-legs ·

Once upon a time, at the edge of a big dark forest, there lived a girl called Masha and her father and stepmother. And that stepmother, well, when her father was there, she smiled and spoke sweet as honey. But when her father was away it was, "Do this, Masha! Do that!" Whatever Masha did, it was never good enough. Sharp words were all she heard.

One day when her father had gone to visit friends in a distant village, her stepmother said, "Tomorrow, Masha, I shall make you a new dress. But first you must go and borrow a needle and thread from my sister who lives in the forest."

"Borrow a needle and thread!" said Masha. She *was* surprised. "There are plenty of needles and a whole lot of thread in the cupboard."

"Don't argue!" said her stepmother. "Just go! And remember to

105

tell my sister I sent you!"

"But how shall I know the way?" asked Masha.

"That's easy," said her stepmother. "Take the path at the back of the house and follow your nose."

Masha was not stupid. She knew her stepmother was trying to get rid of her. Who lived in the forest? Only the wolf . . . and the bear . . . *and* Baba Yaga Bony-legs, the old Russian witch. But what could she do? She knew she had to go.

So she combed her golden hair, twisted it into a long thick plait and tied it with a bright red ribbon. Then she asked her stepmother for some food for the journey. Her stepmother gave her a lump of stale bread and a bone with only a tiny scrap of meat left on it. That was all. But Masha took the food and wrapped it in an old cotton kerchief that had belonged to her own mother. And then she set off.

She took the path through the forest, straight ahead. She walked and she walked, one foot in front of the other, until she was so tired she had to sit down on a tree stump and rest.

While she was sitting there, a grey mouse came creeping out from under a bush and sniffed the air.

"You look hungry," said Masha; and she opened her kerchief, broke off some breadcrumbs and scattered them on the ground.

When the mouse had eaten the crumbs, he looked up and said, "Girl with the golden hair, why are you walking alone through the dark forest?"

"My stepmother has sent me to borrow a needle and thread from her sister who lives in the forest," said Masha.

"Ahhh . . ." sighed the mouse. "She is sending you to Baba Yaga Bony-legs . . . but you are a girl with a kind heart . . . so don't be afraid . . ." And he whisked his tail and was gone.

Masha wrapped the bone and the rest of the bread in her kerchief, and she walked on.

After a while she came to some birch trees which grew very close together. She walked on, and she came to a clearing in the forest, and *oh!* in the middle of the clearing there was a hut with staring windows, perched on top of two great chicken's legs. And the hut was turning round and round, round and round.

Masha drew herself up, tall and straight as she could, and she said, "Little house, little house, stand with back to forest and face to me!"

And the hut stood still.

Now there was a high gate and a fence of sharp-pointed stakes around the clearing, and when Masha opened the gate it gave a loud C-R-E-A-K!

"Gate," she said, as she closed it behind her, "you need some oil on your hinges!"

She walked towards the hut and a really skinny-looking dog came bounding towards her, barking furiously.

"You look hungry," said Masha; and she opened her kerchief, took out the bone and gave it to him.

And the dog stopped barking, picked up the bone and set to work on it.

Masha walked on. She stepped into the hut on chicken's legs, and there was Baba Yaga, the old witch herself. She was weaving, and the loom was going *clickety-clack! clickety-clack!* And—my goodness!—she was HUGE, with long bony legs and a mouth full of iron teeth.

"Who are you?" she snarled. "And who sent you?"

"My name is Masha," she answered. "And my stepmother, your sister, sent me to borrow a needle and thread."

"To borrow a needle and thread . . . *hmmm* . . . I know what that means!" said Baba Yaga. "Now while I get ready, you must work. Just do the weaving, while I go to the bath house and take a bath. Then it will be time for me to have my supper!" And off she went.

Masha began to weave—*clickety-clack! clickety clack!*—and after a while a thin black cat came strolling into the house.

"You look hungry," said Masha, and she reached for her kerchief, took out the stale bread and gave it to him.

The cat ate every little bit, and when he had finished, he looked up and said, "This is not a good place to be. You must run away before Baba Yaga returns and eats you with her iron teeth."

"But surely she will chase me and catch me?" said Masha.

"On the table," said the cat, "there is a comb and an embroidered towel. Take them, and if Baba Yaga catches up with you in the forest, first throw down the towel and then the comb."

"But what about the weaving? As soon as the clickety-clacking stops, she will be out of the bath house and after me before I can reach the gate."

"I shall do the weaving," said the cat.

"Thank you, good cat," said Masha, and she picked up the towel and the comb. "Now—there is one more thing I must do before I leave." And she picked up a bottle of oil that was standing beside Baba Yaga's lamp.

Meanwhile the cat began to work at the loom. But he had no idea how to weave, and in no time at all he had got the threads twisted and tangled. What a mess and muddle he made of it! But he still kept the loom going *clickety-clack! clickety-clack!*

When Masha stepped out of Baba Yaga's hut, the dog came bounding up to her and licked her hand and wagged his tail. When she came to the gate, she poured the oil on its hinges, and she opened it and it didn't creak.

But when she came to the birch trees, they stretched out their branches and caught hold of her and would not let her pass. So Masha undid the ribbon at the bottom of her golden plait and tied a big floppy bow round one of the branches. And the birch trees lifted their branches, rustled their leaves and let Masha pass.

Then she ran—and ran—and ran.

When Baba Yaga came out of the bath house, she heard the loom clacking, so she didn't hurry. She called through the window, "Are you weaving, my little dear?"

"Yes, auntie," replied the cat, trying to talk like Masha. But his voice came out sort of squeaky, and Baba Yaga knew immediately that it was the cat.

She strode into the house, picked up a ladle and flung it at him. "Why did you let Masha leave?" she snarled. "Why didn't you scratch out her eyes?"

The cat curled up his tail, humped up his back and said, "For years and years I have served you, and you've never even given me a burnt crust. But Masha gave me her own bread."

Out went Baba Yaga. Stamp! stamp!

"Dog, why did you let Masha leave?" she snarled. "Why didn't you bark and bite her?"

The dog looked her straight in the eye and said, "For years and years I have served you, and you've never even given me a dry old bone. But Masha gave me a fresh bone with meat on it."

On went Baba Yaga. Stamp! stamp!

"Gate, why did you let Masha leave?" she snarled. "Why didn't you creak?"

The gate said, "For years and years I have served you, and you have done nothing for me. But Masha bathed my hinges with oil."

Baba Yaga opened the gate and went through. Stamp! stamp!

"Birch trees, why did you let Masha leave?" she snarled. "Why didn't you catch hold of her with your branches?"

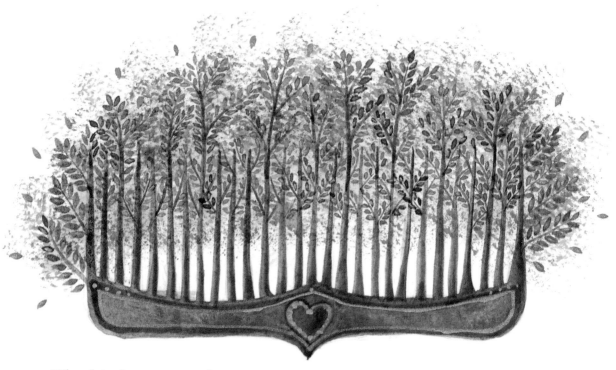

The birch trees said, "For years and years we have served you, and you haven't even tied a piece of string on us. But Masha took her own bright ribbon and tied it on a branch."

Then Baba Yaga jumped into her stone mortar, picked up the pestle and, using it to drive her forward, she was off, through the forest . . . *whoo-oosh!*

As soon as Masha heard the noise, she looked back, and when she saw Baba Yaga on the path behind her, she threw down the towel. And there sprang up a great wide river, brimful of water.

Baba Yaga's mortar was too heavy to float across, so she turned back. She found her cattle, drove them to the river and they drank and drank, until the water was gone. Then she was on her way again . . . *whoo-oosh!*

Masha heard the noise, and when she saw Baba Yaga coming, she threw down the comb. And there sprang up a great host of tall trees, hundreds and thousands of them, so close together it would have been hard for a fly to creep between.

Baba Yaga sharpened her iron teeth. She bit into a tree and hurled it aside. She sharpened her teeth, bit into another tree and hurled it aside. On and on she went. Sharpening, biting and hurling. But the trees were so many and so close that she could not get through, and in the end, shouting and snarling, she turned round and went home.

And Masha? Well, she ran—and ran—and ran.

It was almost dark by the time she got to the edge of the forest. The lamps were lit in her house, and her father was standing outside, looking for her.

"Where have you been?" he called out when he saw her. "What happened? I have been looking for you everywhere."

Masha answered, "Stepmother sent me to her own sister in the forest to borrow a needle and thread, and that sister was Baba Yaga Bony-legs, the witch. It was hard to escape. But some friends helped me, and I managed at last."

When her father heard this, he was angry and strode into the house. But her stepmother had gone.

She had seen Masha and heard everything. She knew she had been found out, and had run off into the forest. And whether she reached the house of her sister, Baba Yaga Bony-legs—or whether the wolf or the bear got her first—no one ever found out.

So that was that. Masha and her father never saw her again. And, from that time on, they lived together in peace and contentment, in their house at the edge of the big dark forest.

Russian

· THE · YELLOW · THUNDER · DRAGON ·

Once, long ago, there was a quiet, thoughtful boy called Chang, who was always day-dreaming—always wishing that something surprising and extraordinary would happen to him. But nothing ever did . . . until one day when he was thirteen years old.

Chang lived with his grandmother and his father, Yin, who was a farmer. Grandmother was special. She was old and wise, and because Chang's mother had died when he was a baby she had looked after him and given him extra love.

Well, one hot afternoon, when Grandmother was asleep and his father was busy in the house, Chang wandered out to the garden gate and looked across the plains and winding river to the mountains beyond. He was quietly day-dreaming when he saw a handsome young man, dressed all in yellow, come riding up the road. Four menservants walked beside him, and one of them held a splendid yellow umbrella over the young man's head to shade him from the sun. There was something strange about these travellers.

Chang watched them carefully. The horse . . . at first sight it looked like a white horse, but as it moved a haze of colour shimmered and shone around it. Like sunshine on water. Chang was sure its hooves didn't touch the ground. And the servants' feet didn't touch the ground either. It was as if they all walked on air.

When the travellers reached the gate, they stopped, and the young man said, "I am weary, Chang, son of Yin. May I enter your father's garden and rest?"

Chang bowed and opened the gate. "Enter, my lord," he said.

The young man swung down from his horse, light and easy, and a servant tethered it to the gatepost. Then they all went and sat down on a seat in the courtyard, next to the house.

As soon as Chang's father heard the sound of voices, he came and welcomed the visitors and asked his son to bring them refreshments. Then he sat down and talked to the handsome young man.

Now while the others ate and drank, Chang stood a little way off, hands tucked in his sleeves and arms folded, watching. There were so many surprising and extraordinary things about these people.

The young man's clothes had no seams. They were woven in one piece. And his feet did not touch the ground when he walked. As for the horse . . . its body was not covered with hair, but with small white shiny scales, and on each scale were five tiny spots of colour.

When the travellers had finished eating and drinking, the young man thanked Yin graciously for his hospitality and the whole party rose and took their leave. And the servant who was carrying the umbrella turned it upside down before crossing the gateway, and when he reached the road, he turned it right side up again.

The handsome young man mounted his horse. He looked at Chang and said, "I shall come again tomorrow."

Chang bowed. "Come, my lord," he answered.

And he stood and watched as they continued up the road towards the mountains. Up and up they went, and then, suddenly, they rose into the air and vanished among the rain clouds that were gathering above the mountains.

When he returned to the house, Chang's father said, "Those were strange visitors. I've never seen that young man before, but he knew my name and everything about me. You were watching them. Did you notice anything unusual?"

"Yes, Father. Their feet and the horse's hooves didn't touch the ground, and besides—"

"Their feet didn't touch the ground!" exclaimed Yin. "Then they were not men. They were spirits. We must tell your grandmother. She knows about these things."

Grandmother was in a deep sleep and didn't want to wake up. But, at last, she stirred and yawned.

"Grandmother," said Chang. "Today we were visited by strangers whose feet did not touch the ground."

Immediately she was wide awake. "Tell me about them," she said.

Then Chang told her about the handsome young man and his yellow seamless clothes, the four servants and the white horse, and how they rose into the air and vanished among the clouds.

"Seamless clothes are magic clothes," said Grandmother. "And yellow is a sacred colour. The young man is the Yellow Thunder Dragon, the horse is a dragon horse, and the servants are the four winds. A great storm will come . . ." She frowned. "Have you told me everything?" she asked.

"There is something else," said Chang. "The servant who was carrying the umbrella turned it upside down before leaving our garden."

"That is a good omen," said Grandmother. And she closed her eyes and once more fell asleep.

In the evening, when Yin looked out and saw dark thunder clouds above the western mountains, he decided that he and Chang should stay up and wait for the storm. In honour of the Yellow Thunder Dragon, Chang put on a yellow robe that his grandmother had made him and lit a yellow lantern; and then he burned incense and read magic charms from an ancient yellow book.

Meanwhile Grandmother slept.

Later that night the storm finally broke. Chang closed his book and he and his father looked out of the window. Lightning flamed. Thunder rolled and boomed. And down came the rain. Swollen streams gushed from the mountains. The river rose higher and higher until at last it burst its banks and flooded the fields, sweeping away everything in its path—trees, houses and all living creatures.

Time passed. The thunder quietened and the lightning moved away. But still the rain came down. As soon as it was light, Yin opened the door and he and Chang looked out; and they could see that the flood water reached right up to their garden.

"We should have fled to the mountains last night," said Yin. "We would have been safe there. But now it is too late."

Then Chang stepped out into the garden and looked up at the sky. Above their house he saw a yellow dragon, with its hood spread out as if to protect them. For one brief moment he saw it—and then it was gone.

"Father!" he cried. "I have seen the Yellow Thunder Dragon!"

"You are tired and dreaming, my son," said Yin.

"But it is not raining on our house!" exclaimed Chang.

And his father went out and saw for himself that, although it was raining everywhere else, no rain fell on their roof.

"So the Thunder Dragon is guarding us," he said. "It was good that you welcomed him and his servants yesterday, my son."

At midday the rain stopped. Only then did Yin and his son realise that, in all the plain, their house alone remained undamaged, as if the storm had never been. The flood waters had come right up to their garden and then swept around it, as if held back by a strong invisible wall.

Later that afternoon the sun came out and Chang went and stood, once again, by the garden gate. He looked to the west and saw the young man, dressed all in yellow and mounted on his white horse, ride down from the mountains with his four servants. And as before, their feet did not touch the ground. At the garden gate the group stopped.

"I told you that I would come again," said the young man. "But this time I shall not enter your garden."

Chang bowed. "As it pleases you," he said.

Then the young man took a scale from the horse's neck and gave it to Chang. "Keep this safely," he said. "And use it wisely."

Chang bowed again.

And the young man and his four servants continued on their way, across the flood water, the horse's hooves and the servants' feet seeming to walk on air. On and on they went, and then, suddenly, they sank down into the water and vanished.

Chang hurried inside and he placed the scale from the horse's neck in a small wooden box, lined with silk. Then he went to his father and told him that the Yellow Thunder Dragon had returned to his pool.

"We must tell Grandmother," said Yin.

Grandmother was *still* asleep. But when at last she stirred and opened her eyes, Chang told her everything that had happened and showed her the small shiny scale.

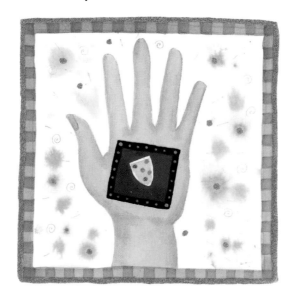

"Now when the emperor sends for you both," said Grandmother, "all will be well."

"And why should the emperor send for us?" asked Yin.

"You shall see," she said. And she closed her eyes and fell asleep.

News travels fast and it was not long before the emperor heard about the storm and the great flood that came with it. He also heard about a strange marvel that had been seen by those who had fled to the mountains to escape the storm. It seemed that rain had not fallen on one house—the house of Yin, the farmer—and the flood waters had swept right round both house and garden, as if they were surrounded by a strong invisible wall.

And the emperor thought there must be some powerful magic at work here, so he sent messengers with orders that Yin and all who lived in the house must come to the imperial palace.

Well, Grandmother refused to go. She said that she felt like sleeping. But Chang and his father set off at once.

It was early evening when they reached the palace. But the emperor received them immediately and asked Yin to tell him what had happened during the storm.

"My lord," said Yin, "the story belongs to my son, Chang. He is the one who must tell it."

So Chang told the story of the Yellow Thunder Dragon from the beginning, and by the time he got to the end it was dark. Then he took the small shiny scale out of the box, and it shone so brightly that it lit the throne room like the noonday sun.

"Chang, son of Yin," said the emperor, "you shall remain here and become one of my royal magicians, for the Yellow Thunder Dragon has given you a scale that holds within it powerful magic."

And so Chang, though he was only thirteen years old, became a royal magician; and as time passed he found that there was indeed powerful magic in the scale from the dragon horse. When he held it in his hand, he could heal the sick. He could foretell the future. He could even win mighty victories for the emperor's army.

And the emperor rewarded Chang generously and gave him a great house near the imperial palace; and his father and grandmother came and lived with him there. His father lived the comfortable life of a rich lord. And Grandmother? Well, she *still* slept most of the time. But when she did wake, she shared with Chang the wisdom and knowledge of her many years.

Chinese

·SOMETHING·ABOUT·THE·STORIES·AND·WHERE·THEY·COME·FROM·

·THE·LEMON·PRINCESS·
It is not always possible to say exactly where a story originated. This popular story has been collected in many countries from Spain through to Turkey and Iran. The Arab domination of much of Spain and Portugal, which lasted about seven hundred years, probably brought the story into that area and from there it doubtless spread throughout southern Europe. The killing of the heroine by a servant girl is a common motif in Arab stories, and the importance of water would seem to indicate an area close to deserts. The magic fruit varies. It can be oranges or even pumpkins. I chose a lemon from the version in *Fairy Tales from Turkey translated by Margery Kent, 1946.*

·FEATHER·WOMAN·AND·THE·MORNING·STAR·
The story of the Star Husband was particularly widespread among North American Indians living in the Plains area. Sometimes the girl reached the sky by climbing into a tree that simply stretched upwards. The moon was regarded by many Indian tribes as a patron of women and of crops. This version is retold from *Walter McClintock: The Old North Trail or Life, Legends and Religion of the Blackfeet Indians, 1910.*

·THE·KINGDOM·UNDER·THE·SEA·
This is a favourite story in Japan. The retelling is based mainly on *F. H. Davis: Myths and Legends of Japan, 1917.* Urashima's lacquer box usually only contains mist or smoke, and he immediately grows old and dies. The motif for the ending, where he finally becomes a crane, appears in a version quoted in *Keigo Seki (translated by Robert J. Adams): Folk-tales of Japan, 1963.*

·UNANANA·AND·THE·ENORMOUS·ONE-TUSKED·ELEPHANT·
Many African tales, like this one, were written down for the first time by white missionaries or administrators. I have taken this story from *Henry Callaway: Nursery Tales, Traditions and Histories of the Zulus in their own Words, 1868.* Elephants make well-defined roads through the bush, and the male when roused and angry is dangerous.

·KATE·CRACKERNUTS·
It is unusual in fairy tale for two step-sisters to be fond of each other and also to share the same name. Only two versions have been collected. One from the Orkney Islands: *Folklore Vol. I (Sept. 1890)* and the other from Angus: *Longman's Magazine Vol. XII (Nov. 1888 to April 1889).* Resourceful, determined girls are found more frequently in Scottish fairy tales than in those from other countries.

·THE·KING·WHO·WANTED·TO·TOUCH·THE·MOON·
This story from Dominica: *Manuel de Andrade: Folklore of the Dominican Republic, 1930,* has travelled from West Africa. In one version, collected in the Congo, the king has a bamboo tower built in order to reach the treasure that is sparkling in the sky.

· THREE · GOLDEN · APPLES ·

The magic fruit can be peaches, oranges, golden apples or figs, while the other brothers' baskets may contain cow pats and horse dung! French fairy tales are particularly lively, inventive and humorous. Dozens of different versions of this story have been collected in France. A typical version is the one in *Revue des Traditions Populaires, Vol. VI, 1891.*

· THE · MAGIC · FRUIT ·

This story was first recorded by Francisco de Avila in 1608. (See *H. B. Alexander: Mythology of all Races Vol. XI, 1920.*) Cavillaca and Coniraya were 'huacas' who lived in the world as humans. Although I have called them great magicians, they were more like spirits or gods. The fruit of the lucuma tree is noted for its sweetness.

· SEVEN · CLEVER · BROTHERS ·

While there are numerous stories, particularly in northern Europe, of travelling companions with amazing skills, this one is unusual with its central emphasis on the importance of seven brothers staying good friends. *G. Friedlander: Jewish Fairy Tales and Stories, 1918.*

· THE · PRINCE · AND · THE · FLYING · CARPET ·

Stealing magic objects by cheating the quarrelsome owners is a motif that occurs widely in fairy tales. Instead of a carpet, bag and stick, there may be a travelling cap, a self-filling purse, and a horn or whistle which, when blown, will summon soldiers. *Maive S. H. Stokes: Indian Fairy Tales, 1879.*

· THE · HALLOWEEN · WITCHES ·

Here a European tale (in an English version a baker's miserly daughter becomes an owl) meets the African 'Conjure Wife' to give a new story typical of Black American folk tale. The retelling is based on two versions: *Martha Young: Plantation Bird Legends, 1916* and *Frances G. Wickes: Holiday Stories, 1921.*

· KOALA ·

Central to this story is the importance of being careful with water in the dry season. From *R. Brough Smyth: The Aborigines of Victoria, 1878.*

· BABA · YAGA · BONY-LEGS ·

No other country has a witch quite like the Russian Baba Yaga. In one story, the fence around her house is made of human bones and on the spikes are human skulls with staring eyes! Retold mainly from *W. R. Ralston: Russian Folk Tales, 1873.*

· THE · YELLOW · THUNDER · DRAGON ·

Chinese dragons are quite different from the European fire-breathing variety. They are associated with water, sleeping in deep pools and emerging to bring rain. They are god-like creatures and can adopt a human form. *Donald A. Mackenzie: Myths of China and Japan, 1923.*